Rubina Chinchada

and the

Enchanted Dresser

A Crafty Chica Novelita

Kathy Cano-Murillo

Edited by Martin Dolan.

This novelita is dedicated to all those who have followed my online (and offline) adventures throughout the years - and anyone who loves happy ghost stories and Día de los Muertos!

Please check out my other novels available in paperback, ebook, and audiobook:

Waking Up in the Land of Glitter

Miss Scarlet's School of Patternless Sewing

Visit my site, CraftyChica.com

For more stories, essays, craft tutorials,

recipes, videos and mas!

Peace, love and glitter!

Kathy

@craftychica on social media

Table of contents

Chapter One

Once a season at sunrise, the residents of the Coronado neighborhood of central Phoenix awoke to rustlings in their front yards. Bulk trash pickup was scheduled for the next morning, which meant that strange crafty girl, Rubina, would be by early to pilfer through their castoffs.

Sure enough, as the sun peeked over the rooftops, Rubina Chinchada cruised down the historic, tree-lined street at 5 miles per hour, peering out the window of her SUV in search of the bedroom dresser of her dreams. Her plans? Embellish it from stem to stern in her signature Mexi-boho style. Her trusty cousin and roommate, Mona, had been enticed to join the quest with an offering of a quad mocha-spice latte.

It sounded like a splendid plan last night as the two decorated sugar skulls for Día de los Muertos, but this morning, Mona struggled to stay awake.

"Rubina Chinchada," Mona said, "Only you would drag me out here at the crack of dawn on Halloween to go dumpster-diving." Rubina picked up the steaming latte from the cup holder and waved it under Mona's nose.

Mona arched one eyebrow and swayed forward to inhale the aroma and then smirked. She took the drink and sipped, scalding her tongue.

"Thanks a lot, prima. ¡híjole! Well, *now* I'm awake. All I'm saying is, why can't we hit up yard sales like normal people? Sneaking up on private property at this ungodly hour feels so criminal. I thought you said 7:30, and you came busting in my room at 5!"

"I know, *sawree*," Rubina replied. "Ever since I went on that stupid Scottsdale Haunted Home Tour last week, I've had weird dreams about a crying lady following me. I can't get a good night's sleep at all. And I can't pinpoint it, but I know I'm meant to visit *this* street *this* morning. My new dresser awaits."

"You gotta stop watching those crazy novelas with your nana," Mona told her. "If it's not that, then maybe it's La Llorona, and she wants you to teach her how to knit."

Rubina and Mona giggled as they stopped at a two-story adobe. Rubina stepped down from her red 4Runner to reach across a heap of yard scraps, garbage-can lids and boxes of old dishes to retrieve a broken lamp. But just as her fingers touched the chipped porcelain, her allergies flared. She sneezed, lost her footing and her lanky frame toppled onto the pile.

It wasn't the sound of clanging knickknacks that woke the homeowner, but Rubina's howl of pain, which easily could have been mistaken for a cat in heat.

"Hey, kid!" an old man shouted from his bedroom window. "Like I told you last time, it's all junk — get lost!" Mona slinked down in her seat, thoroughly embarrassed as usual. All this for the sake of crafting, Mona thought. Girl needs a glue-gun intervention...

Rubina's mom, a prude non-creative, never appreciated her daughter's innovation and forbid all manners of craftiness, which she considered tacky. Rubina rebelled by igniting a handmade revolution everywhere she went. But instead of fires and flags, she used gems and sequins — daily. Mona often worried Rubina, someday, would meet her match.

"Rubina, I'm done. Let's go," Mona complained.

"We're not dumpster-diving — we're *fronster* diving," Rubina corrected her cousin as she picked dead leaves off her sugar-skull-embellished sweater. "People set out their eclectic miscellany so prolific artists like me can give it new life."

Rubina pumped the lamp over her head and whisper-yelled to the man's window. "Pssst, any chance you have the partner for this?"

Mona revved the 4Runner's engine. Rubina sighed, chucked the lamp back onto the pile and climbed aboard. She had spent the last month remodeling her room: A wood burned headboard with angels, a wall tricked out with stenciled Chihuahuas, and her favorite, a gold-glitter floor. All she needed was a wow-factor vanity that popped with personality.

No store in town could provide that. Why couldn't Mona understand?

"I need to find a dresser ASAP," Rubina said. "This morning, all my clean clothes slid off my elliptical. Second day in a row."

Mona nodded. "Fine, but remember, I have to be at my sister's by noon."

"I can't believe you offered to babysit overnight on Halloween and leave me all alone in the house," Rubina said. She then noticed a pretty orange butterfly flitter across the street and disappear into the flowerbed of a giant crimson house with an enormous carport — in which sat a single piece of chunky furniture.

"That's it, there's my dresser!" Rubina squealed. "Feel my arms, Mona, I just got the chills!" In all her 23 years, Rubina had never spotted such trash-to-treasure gold. The find was an antique wooden vanity dresser, complete with a tri-fold mirror, all of it trimmed in carved rose vines. For an obsessive, experienced craftaholic like herself, Rubina knew this was the holy grail of dumpster-div ... er, *fronster* diving.

Rubina scooted out of her vinyl seat, slammed the car door and immediately began the inspection, which lasted all of three seconds. "It looks like it's from the 1920s or '30s. The surface is raw enough so I don't even need to prime it."

Mona scratched her head of frizzy chestnut curls and climbed out of the vehicle onto the slick, grassy lawn. She clenched her sweater under her chin, shuffling along in her corduroy slippers. "You promised I wouldn't have to get out of the car. Sheesh, it's freezing all of a sudden."

Rubina spun around, irritated. "Can you please stop being a creativity blocker for, like, five minutes, and just help?" Rubina swooped her arms in front of the dresser to showcase it to her cousin. "Isn't it beautiful? Listen closely. Can't you hear these carved roses crying for a coat of bright fuchsia acrylic, sealed with glitter varnish?" She lovingly ran her fingers along the border of the mirrors. "And I could cover all of this with Nana's costume-jewelry collection. Bathroom caulk works wonders as industrial adhesive!"

Mona opened the back of the SUV, and then assisted Rubina with dragging the antique across the concrete of the carport. The young women flinched at the annoying scratchy sound.

"Do you have to decorate every thing, Rubina?," asked Mona. "I'm still a little pissed about my toilet-seat lid. Hey, I made a pun! Ha! Anyway...I never said I wanted it covered in bottle caps. Do you know how many scratches I have on my nalgas now? Craftastrophe if you ask me. Prima, this dresser is perfect as is. It would be disrespectful to alter it."

Mona dropped her end of the dresser when she spotted the homeowner, her hair up in pink foam rollers, tending a massive succulent garden on the side of the house. The poodle at the woman's side zipped across the yard to yap at the girls.

"You don't want this, right?" Rubina hollered, gesturing to the dresser while keeping one eye on the hyper pooch.

"Take it, please! And promise not to bring it back," the woman replied.

Rubina chuckled and thought, "As if!" This old-school baby was meant to be the crown jewel of her decor. "Of course," she told the homeowner, who had hustled over to scoop up her pooch.

The old woman stood up tall. "I'm serious. We never want to see that heap of wood again." Her poodle barked once, as if to agree.

Mona and Rubina exchanged puzzled glances. Why such an ominous reply? Mona folded her arms across her chest and shivered, her teeth chattering from the cold. She opened the top drawer with one finger.

"This thing is creepy," she said. "It has a logo from a freakin' coffin company!" Mona backed away. "Eww. What if it was dug up from a cemetery or something?"

No way, Rubina thought. But sure enough, inside the drawer was an embossed logo: Monarch Coffin Company.

Rubina bent over, swooped her bobbed black hair behind her ears and knelt before the dresser. It still smelled of pine. "Um, by any chance, did this dresser used to be a coffin?" she asked jokingly out of the side of her mouth.

The old woman decked out in her fuzzy teal slippers and a red silk kimono said nothing as she locked the entryway gate and retreated inside her home, slamming the front door.

"I don't want this thing in our house, cuz," Mona muttered. "I'm not kidding. Let's go."

"You owe me, Mona Garcia. Does the Great Bed Bug Scare of 2010 ring a bell? This is nothing compared to that. We're taking the dresser," Rubina said. She then rolled up her sleeves and, with all their might, the cousins pushed the dresser into the back of the SUV. "Just wait and see. I'll give this baby a royal makeover. Good vibes, I promise. All it's missing is a little love."

Chapter Two

Rubina face-planted on her bed, every ounce of energy spent. She had just devoted 12 straight hours to the dresser, and nothing had gone as planned.

Earlier, she had dropped Mona off to babysit, then made a pit stop at the craft store, shelling out $90 on paints, varnish, glitter, crystals and three types of super-strength glues. She turned off the porch light; no time for trick-or-treaters tonight!

But that joy swiftly turned to annoyance. With the dresser in her bedroom, Rubina lined her work area with newspaper. She painted the dresser black, the carved roses hot pink and the leaves green. But as fast as she could apply the acrylics, they seemed to evaporate, like water on wax paper. Rubina never cried over a craft project gone wrong, but right now, she wanted to bust a tear.

"I bet the varnish is so old, it's seeped into the wood. I need an industrial sander," Rubina thought with a sigh. She decided to leave the original wood finish, just add glittered accents. That didn't work either.

In the hours that followed, Rubina tried everything she knew to get something, anything to stick on the aged dresser. She even phoned the craft store to complain that the products were defective. By 10 p.m., she burst into a series of whines that went far beyond the frustration of a normal craft fail.

A surge of gloom washed over her spirit and she couldn't shake it. Why did she feel so bad over a crusty old piece of furniture?

Finally, she called it a night. She picked up all her paints and set them neatly on top of the dresser. First thing in the morning, she'd get back to work. For now, she'd crash. She stared at the dresser and saluted. "Tomorrow, *I* rule."

Just as she leaned over to click off the glass mosaic lamp, a something whooshed by her head. Rubina dodged it just in time. Before she could catch her breath, she heard a loud thunk, just inches from her face. She froze in confusion as she watched a glob of emerald paint drip down her wall of stenciled Chihuahuas.

Now she was angry! Those stenciled designs took an entire weekend to complete! What the heck was going on here? She searched the room for clues and noted a busted jar on the floor. How in the world could it have flown all the way from the dresser, across the room? And with such force?

Nervous, but in denial of anything supernatural, Rubina cleaned up the mess and remained calm, even though her insides shivered. She said a prayer to her deceased abuelo for protection. Rubina figured with her lack of sleep, and the marathon but unsuccessful craft session, she was simply delirious. She clicked off the light and snuggled under the bedspread, wishing she had turned on the heater. Her room felt chillier than a skating rink.

Then a paint bottle dropped. Then another. And another. One-by-one, off the dresser and onto the glittered floor. *This was real.* Someone — or something — was in her bedroom, taunting her. As much as Rubina wanted to jump up and bolt the room, her body lay like a stone on her bed, 100 percent numb.

Then she heard it.

Faintly — yet somehow loud all the same — a woman wept. In front of the ... dresser?

"OK, *now* I know why that lady in the rollers wanted to ditch this thing," Rubina thought. "It's possessed!" She scrunched her face tight and slid down to try to disappear under the patchwork comforter. With every passing second, the cries grew into sobs, each more sorrowful than the last. Whatever was there wanted Rubina to notice.

She turned on her side. Carefully, she reached down to her nightstand, picked up her craft caddy and slid it under her arm. Surely there was something in there she could use for defense.

Rubina blinked hard, then opened her eyes. An apparition of a young curvy woman in a vintage lacy slip stood tall in front of the mirror, stroking her mane of silky ebony hair with Rubina's brush! She felt the same overwhelming sense of gloom as earlier. The woman had to be about Rubina's age — early 20s — her face frowned with sadness from her eyes to her chin.

The ghost peered into the mirror and made eye contact with Rubina; piercing her soul like an ice pick. This was the woman who had haunted Rubina's dreams all week!

"Oh my God," Rubina thought, "she must have latched on to me from that haunted-house tour!"

The woman placed her ghostly hands on the top of the dresser; they appeared to pass through the wood. "It's mine … leave it alone," she said, still looking at Rubina in the mirror.

Rubina crept to the corner of her bed like a spider. "Sweet baby Jesus in a manger, she's talking to me! This ghost is creeping on me, what do I do?" she said in a panicked whisper. She dove under the comforter and grabbed the craft caddy. A can, she felt a can, it would have to do. She emerged from her bunker.

Ever so cautiously.

"Bury it for me..." the woman pleaded, hovering in mid-air, her face mere millimeters from Rubina's.

Rubina leapt up and sprayed high-gloss varnish at the apparition, to no effect. Rubina chucked several skeins of yarn at her, followed by crochet needles she flung like darts.

The woman floated about the room, swirling around Rubina, chanting "It's mine ... it's mine ... *it's mine!*"

"I'm sorry I took your dresser, I don't want it anymore, *leave me alone*! You're *dead*! It's Halloween, go haunt a graveyard or something!"

The spirit backed away.

"Cross over!" Rubina shouted at her, trying to remember all the stuff she had seen on "A Haunting" on the Discovery Channel. "Go to the light! Go back to Scottsdale!"

It worked. The woman vanished as soon as Rubina flipped on the light.

Rubina panted, bolted the room, shut the door and shoved a chair under the doorknob. She grabbed her purse, keys and travel yarn bag and left for her parents' house for refuge.

Thank goodness for the comforts of her mom's sugar-cookie candles, leftover pizza, and the *Gilmore Girls* marathon! She curled up on the comfy family room couch, still trembling a bit, and rang Mona.

The girls dissected each moment of the past 24 hours until sunlight crept through the windows. Mona couldn't leave her sister's until 8 a.m., but she did her best to console her cousin.

Finally, Rubina, weary and sleepy, made her way home and felt confident enough to confront the dresser. There in the early morning sunlight, Rubina marched in the house like an angry lumberjack, grabbed the haunted antique, and dumped it on the sidewalk.

Rubina sighed in relief and dusted her hands the way one does when a tough project is finished. For the first time in days, she felt ready to sleep long and hard. She let her head drop back and listened the sweetness of the chirping birds. She then inhaled the morning air and grinned. What a night! Thank God it's over. She would never visit or watch anything dealing with hauntings again. She would think twice before revamping vintage items. Her bubble of clarity popped when she heard a truck roll up in front of her house. Two tattooed chicks in flannel shirts and skinny jeans jumped out, impressed by the dresser.

"This thing is sick, I need it," one of them said as she shooed away a nosy orange butterfly. "So gothic. We can refinish the top and it'll be perfect for the living room."

"They're really putting this out for bulk trash?" the other asked, opening and shutting each drawer.

Rubina had known this might happen, which is why she quickly made a sign, ran outside and tape it to the vanity's distressed mirror:

BEWARE: TERMITES!

Chapter Three

Hours later, Rubina awoke on the sectional to her ringtone. She fumbled for her cell and, before she could say a word, Mona started in.

"Rubina! Did you check your voicemail or your email? Never mind — did you put the dresser out? If you did, go save it! Don't let the bulk trash get it, we gotta keep it!"

"Loca, are you on crack? I'm not touching that thing, lesson learned," Rubina replied, grumpy for being roused from her much-needed slumber.

"My uncle is driving me home right now. Go get the dresser!"

"Why?"

"Because I Googled Monarch Coffin Company. They're still in business! I just hung up with the owner and told him what happened. There's a juicy love story behind it! I explained it in the email, but go get the dresser first! Trust me! Please, Rubina. I know I was against this whole thing, but now I'm involved!

"Go get the dresser!!"

Click.

Rubina laughed and peered through the blinds; the dresser was still there, intact. No way, even if her vintage rhinestone collection depended on it, would she bring that piece of frightful furniture back in the house. She powered up her laptop and bounced her foot up and down while the new emails loaded.

Rubina — I looked up Monarch Coffin Company, they're still in business! The owner knows all about the dresser, it belonged to his grandfather, Duarte Mendez! He built it for his fiancé, Isabella Cruz, in the late 1920s. Her family was from Scottsdale and they were crazy rich. They hated Duarte because he was a lowly carpenter. Isabella and Duarte were secretly engaged until she got pneumonia. He carved beautiful rose-trimmed pine coffins for him and for her so they could be together in the afterlife. But when she died, her parents ditched the coffin and bought a fancy one. They forbid him to attend her funeral. Duarte went crazy and made a dresser out of her coffin for his bedroom. That's how Monarch Coffins began. The tale is that she would come visit him every night as long as he had the dresser. One day, his house burned to the ground and everyone assumed the dresser was destroyed. Supposedly there have been sightings, but no one knows for sure. It's been an urban legend ever since. No one knows where Isabella is buried, her parents kept it a secret from Duarte, but honestly – I think she's the ghost you saw!

Monarch wants to buy the dresser from us. Hopefully you will have saved it by now, if not, get your butt out there!
XO, Mona

Rubina sat up straight. This was better than *any* of Nana's novelas. It all made sense; no wonder Isabella didn't want her dresser covered with costume jewelry. Poor thing! And last night was the start of Día de Los Muertos, the beloved 3,000 year-old Mexican tradition when the departed return to visit their loved ones for an evening. Isabella returned to where her heart belonged, with Duarte!

Mona's last words swept through Rubina's head.

Rubina ran outside to save Isabella's coffin-turned-dresser. But the moment she stepped through the door, she saw the rusty jaws of a front-end loader scoop it up.

"Wait! Please, wait!" she screamed to the loader's operator as she sprinted barefoot onto the driveway. The operator adjusted his headphones and waved cheerily to Rubina. "Thank God, just in time!" she thought.

Not quite. The jaws gripped the dresser. Rubina put her hands to her face.

CRUNCH!

And just like that — Isabella and Duarte's dresser was reduced to firewood and dumped in the back of a trash truck.

Chapter Four

Rubina never went back to sleep. She and Mona spent the rest of the day crafting with all their heart and soul. They packed up their masterpieces and drove to St. Francis Cemetery.

There, with the moonlight shining on their happy faces, among the tall oak trees and concrete benches, the cousins were ready to make peace with Isabella. It wasn't an easy feat to find her grave. But thanks to Google and a chain of phone calls, they discovered Isabella's parents secretly registered it under the name of her Tia's cousin: Xiomara Castillo. They assumed to prevent the grave from being discovered by her forbidden love, Duarte Mendez.

The strong scent of marigolds wafted through the graveyard as a large family walked by carrying a wreath, lighted candles and a sugar dusted pan de muerto. Mona and Rubina's hearts melted as they watched the parents and kids stop at a headstone and lovingly arrange the items atop the grassy lawn. Rubina and Mona were about to do the same, because they finally had located Isabella's plot.

"Isabella Cruz, my name is Rubina Chinchada, and this my cousin, Mona Garcia. We're here on this beautiful, clear night of Día de Los Muertos at your grave to pledge our friendship. I am so sorry that I threw my yarn at you last night ... and sprayed you with varnish, I've never been visited by a ghost before. I freaked out a little; please forgive me."

Mona cleared her throat. *"Annnd?"*

"And I want to apologize for trying to decorate your coffin with glitter. And that it got demolished by the bulk-trash guy. I should have listened to Mona and saved your dresser before reading her email."

Rubina's phone vibrated in her pocket. She winked at Mona and ran across the grass, down the sidewalk to the cemetery's parking lot. In the meantime, Mona shifted her weight from one foot to the other and decided to have her own conversation with Isabella.

"Hi, Isabella! Mona here. Rubina will be right back. I know this isn't much, but we did manage to scoop up a few pieces from your beloved coffin. I used two of them to make a little cross and Rubina wood burned your name across the center. It's really pretty. She kinda takes after Duarte; she's quite handy with her woodworking skills!"

Minutes later, Rubina returned, out of breath, and said, "It's time!" Mona stepped back so Rubina could take center stage.

"Isabella," she began, her voice cracking. "We have someone here to see you."

The girls stepped aside so Andy Mendez, a handsome young man, could maneuver an elderly man in a shiny red wheelchair to Isabella's grave.

Andy greeted each girl with a kiss on the cheek and introduced his great-grandfather, Duarte Mendez. "He's pretty tired these days, he's 101," he said as he locked the wheels of the chair. "Tata Duarte, are you sure you're up for this?"

Tata Duarte swatted his hand at his great-grandson. "Not at all. I've waited decades for this moment!"

Rubina chuckled, tears racing down her cheeks. She couldn't believe Duarte was right here. All because of the dresser she found — or did it find her? It didn't matter. She hoped it would bring Isabella peace. Mona bent over and hugged Duarte with all her might. Rubina leaned in and clasped her soft hands around his wrinkled ones.

"Mr. Mendez, your furniture pieces are exquisite and breathtaking, I'm so honored to have been a collector. Even if it was only for a few hours."

"I only made one," he said. "In honor of my first love, Isabella. She designed it on paper and nagged me to build it, but I never had time. It wasn't until she passed that I made it in her honor ... and then I lost it ... and her."

His lip trembled as he lowered his head.

Rubina kneeled at his feet and lifted his chin with her hand. "Look at me, Mr. Mendez. You mean everything to her. She loves it and she loves you. I know she is very happy you are here right now." Rubina felt Andy's hands upon her shoulders. Maybe this was closure for him, too.

Tata Duarte stuck a shaky hand inside his jacket and retrieved a small sugar skull wrapped in a polka dot napkin, a single fresh marigold, a pink handkerchief and a picture of the two of them together so many years ago. He handed them to Andy, who placed them on Isabella's headstone. Rubina and Mona opened their basket and pulled out a large sugar skull emblazed with hot pink foil, sequins, icing and a ribbon across the forehead that said "RIP Isabella Cruz." They set out a string of papel picado, a row of prayer candles, a plate of chicken mole, and even more fresh marigolds.

The girls kissed the calavera confection and placed it next to Tata Duarte's offerings. Just then, a little orange butterfly flew around, above and then between each of them before landing on Tata's Duarte's shoulder. Water filled his eyes as he let out a robust laugh and watched.

"She loved monarch butterflies", he said, admiring the insect. A youthful smile spread across his face from ear to ear, his eyes shining with delight and comfort. "Because orange was her favorite color". The beautiful insect fluttered its wings, brushed across his cheek, and then gracefully flew away, high into the sky. Tata Duarte closed his eyes and whispered "Mil gracias" under his breath.

Rubina gasped and covered her mouth. That little butterfly had been with her through this whole ordeal, but she'd never noticed until now.

"It's Isabella," Rubina whispered. "Her spirit is set free"

Mona put her arm around her cousin. "Yo se. It sure is. She's finally at peace thanks to you and your addiction to crafts. Sooo, did you learn your lesson about fronster diving, cuz?"

"Yes," Rubina replied. "After all this, I learned I want to do it more than ever!"

About the Author

Kathy Cano-Murillo is an author, artist & founder of the award-winning site, CraftyChica.com. She loves to spread the gospel of glitter — literally through her DIY projects and figuratively through her speeches, workshops, books, and essays. A former reporter for *The Arizona Republic*, she is now a full-time writer, artist and product designer which has led to partnerships with Coca-Cola, HSN, HP, WordPress, Disney & many others. She has authored seven craft books and two novels, and has been featured in *The New York Times*, *USA Today*, *Huffington Post*, *Buzzfeed* + more. Her "Mexi-boho" art and product lines have been carried in hundreds of shops across the country. Kathy is Mexican-American, a native Phoenician, mom of two, a wife, and has five Chihuahuas!

Made in the USA
Las Vegas, NV
20 October 2021